THE AFTER SCHOOL SECRET

by Linda Barr

illustrated by Estella Hickman

To my husband Tom, my son Danny, and especially to my daughter Colleen, who helps me remember what it's like to be a fifth grader.

Published by Willowisp Press, Inc.
401 E. Wilson Bridge Road, Worthington, Ohio 43085

Copyright © 1987 by Willowisp Press, Inc.

Printed in the United States of America

10 9 8 7 6 5 4 3 2 1

ISBN 0-87406-230-6

One

"I can't believe it," Lianne muttered under her breath. "She forgot her line again!"

Lianne slouched down in her seat in the front row of the auditorium. She watched Jenny, who was kneeling in the center of the stage. Jenny's blond hair almost touched the stage as she pretended to scrub the floor. But Lianne could see that under all that hair, Jenny was looking pleadingly toward Mrs. Monk.

But I haven't finished the floor, Stepmother, thought Lianne.

"But I haven't. . ." whispered Mrs. Monk, who was standing off to one side of the stage.

"Oh! Right! But I haven't finished the floor,

Mother," said Jenny quickly.

STEPmother! Lianne said to herself in disgust. Why didn't Mrs. Monk choose me to be Cinderella? she thought. I'm the one who already knew all the lines! Lianne thought back to the day three weeks before, when Mrs. Monk picked the cast for the fifth-grade play. She could still hear one of the kids she thought was a friend whisper to someone, "Lianne just doesn't look like Cinderella."

Lianne pulled on her thick black braid and frowned at her playbook. Her lines were marked with a yellow highlighter. She'd gotten the part of Esmeralda, the ugly stepsister!

If only Mom and Dad were really my parents, Lianne thought. Then maybe I'd have blond hair and light skin, too. Or maybe I'd look like my sister Amy. Her curly brown hair makes her look like Mom, and her blue eyes are like Dad's. Everyone always thinks Amy belongs to Mom and Dad, until they find out she's adopted, too. But they know right away I'm different. "What country are you from, Lianne?" kids ask. "China or Japan?" Most of them have never even heard of Vietnam.

"That's enough for today," called Mrs. Monk. "We'll start with the second act tomorrow. Practice your lines, everyone!"

Lianne sighed and grabbed her books and jacket. She slipped out the side door of the auditorium. She didn't even wait to walk home with Bess, who was her best friend for three years and the other ugly stepsister in the play. Lianne just didn't feel like talking to anyone right now. She decided to take the long way home.

Her feet shuffled through the crunchy leaves. The wind was getting chilly. Lianne put on her fuzzy pink jacket and zipped it up just as she reached the little park on the corner of her street.

The park was empty. But as Lianne slowly walked through the leaves, she thought she heard a child's voice. She stopped and turned toward the swings. One of the swings moved a little in the wind.

"Must be my imagination," she mumbled to herself. She passed the rusty trash barrel on the corner. There it was again! Lianne looked quickly at the jungle gym. No one was in sight!

Then she heard it again, louder this time. It sounded like it was coming from the trash barrel! Lianne stood on her tiptoes and peeked inside. The papers in the barrel were moving, but she couldn't see what was under them.

Then a furry little face popped out from under a crumpled newspaper. A kitten looked at her with sad eyes! Lianne dropped her books and grabbed the trash barrel. She tugged on it until it tipped on its side. Then she pushed the papers and junk out of the way. She finally reached the frightened kitten and lifted it out of the barrel.

"Mew! Mew! Mew!" the kitten cried. Lianne held it tightly against her chest and petted its soft gray fur. The kitten clung to her jacket with sharp little claws. Its face, legs, and tail were a darker gray than its body.

"I bet you're hungry!" Lianne said gently. Then

she picked up her books and stuffed them under her arm. "Come on. I'll get you something to eat. You're just too skinny!" The kitten stopped holding on so tightly and began to purr. It looked up at Lianne and she saw that one eye was blue and one was green.

Lianne hurried up the sidewalk to her house and walked quickly up the front steps. This is good timing, she thought. Mom said she might be a little late getting home from work. She won't find out about you just yet. She always says no more pets. Lianne smiled at the kitten cuddled in her arms.

It's a good thing Amy always stays at Mrs. Graft's house when Mom's late, Lianne thought. I don't think Amy could keep you a secret!

Lianne opened the front door of her house. Once she was inside, she headed straight for the kitchen. "You know," she told the kitten, "I'm hungry, too!"

Then Boomer, the family poodle, raced around the corner. The kitten screeched and climbed up

Lianne's jacket onto her shoulder. Its claws went right into Lianne's skin.

"Ouch!" Lianne yelled. She tried to unhook the kitten's claws from her shoulder, but the kitten just kept hanging on.

Boomer cocked his head and stared at the noisy kitten. Lianne grabbed the poodle's collar and shut him in the bathroom. Finally the kitten stopped screeching and let go of Lianne's jacket.

Lianne held the kitten against her chest and looked into the refrigerator. "Hey, here's just what you need! Fish!" She set the cat on the floor and pulled out a heavy package wrapped in white paper. The label said "perch." "You'll love perch!" The kitten suddenly began mewing loudly.

When Boomer heard the kitten, he started yelping from behind the bathroom door. "Boy, I'm glad Mom can't hear this!" Lianne said.

Lianne put the whole package on the floor and ripped open the thick paper. She pulled off a little strip of fish. The kitten gobbled it right down. She tore off five or six more pieces and fed them to the eager little cat. Finally the kitten stopped eating and began to lick its paws.

"You know, kitty, if you stay with me, you can have fish every day!" Lianne sat cross-legged on the floor and pulled the cat into her lap.

"Now, what can I call you? How about Fluffy?" Lianne petted the little cat. "Well, you're soft, but not very fluffy. How about Muffy? Yeah, that's it!"

Lianne held the kitten up so she could see its face. "I've got to find a way to keep you, Muffy! I'll show Mom you won't be any trouble at all!"

Just then Lianne heard a car turn into their driveway.

Two

LIANNE grabbed the kitten and rushed it out the back door. She heard a car door close with a thud. I've got to hurry! she thought. She snatched up the torn package of fish and folded the paper wrapper up as best as she could. She shoved it in the refrigerator just as the front door opened. Lianne could hear Amy's voice.

". . . and she said it was the best one in the whole first grade!"

"That's great, Amy. Lianne, we're home!" her mother called. "Lianne? Boomer?" Lianne suddenly realized Boomer was still shut in the bathroom! He was barking his head off.

"Oh, hi, Mom," Lianne called from the kitchen.

She tried to sound casual while she quickly opened the bathroom door. The poodle rushed out, still yelping.

"What's wrong with Boomer?" Lianne's mom asked as she came into the kitchen. She picked up the panting dog. "Why is he so excited?"

"He's just glad to see you, Mom." Lianne hoped she wasn't panting like the dog.

Mrs. Bennett put the poodle down to stop him from licking her face.

Amy wandered into the kitchen. She was admiring a big sheet of paper. The paper had lots of orange and brown paint on it.

"Let me see it again, Amy," Mrs. Bennett said. With a big smile Amy handed the picture to her mom.

"An 'Excellent'! I told you she would like it," Mrs. Bennett said. "Let's put it on the refrigerator."

Lianne watched as her mother taped the picture to the front of the refrigerator. Amy's picture now covered the math test Lianne had brought home the day before. That was an 'Excellent' too, she thought.

"How was school today, Lianne? Did you have play practice again?"

Lianne nodded. "Jenny still doesn't know her lines," she said.

Lianne could feel her mother watching her. "You'd make a great Cinderella, honey. I think all the girls would like to be Cinderella. But only one can play the part. You'll be the best Esmeralda ever!" Mrs. Bennett gave Lianne a hug. "I have to go change clothes. Would you get out the package of fish that's in the refrigerator?"

As soon as her mother disappeared up the stairs, Lianne rushed to the kitchen window. Muffy was nowhere in sight. What if Muffy ran away?

But in the meantime, what was she going to do about the fish? Lianne got the package out and opened it again. She poked the fish, trying to make it look whole. Then she heard her mother's voice behind her.

"You know, I'm sure I bought more fish than that," Mrs. Bennett said in a puzzled voice.

"I ate some for a snack!" Lianne said cheerfully.

"Raw?" asked her mother.

"No, I cooked it. In the microwave!"

"Instead of eating cookies?"

Lianne could tell her mother didn't quite believe her. "We're learning about nutrition in science class," Lianne said with a bright smile. "Fish is really good for you!"

Her mother looked at her closely and sighed. "I guess there's enough left to make a casserole."

"That'll be good!" Lianne said quickly. "Can I go over to Bess's house? Maybe we'll go to the park?"

"I guess so." Her mother was still staring at the fish. "Be back in half an hour, okay?"

As soon as Lianne closed the front door behind her, she started whispering, "Here, kitty. Here, Muffy!" Oh, please! Lianne begged. Let Muffy still be here!

14

Three

AFTER a minute or two Lianne heard a little rustling noise behind a bush. She turned just as the kitten jumped out and ran to her.

Hurray! Lianne thought. She looked around to make sure no one was watching. Then she stuffed the kitten inside her jacket and zipped it halfway up. Trying not to hurry, she walked back past the park to Bess's house. Lianne forced herself not to smile. She didn't want to give away her secret.

Wait till Bess sees Muffy! Lianne thought excitedly. She wants a cat even more than I do!

Bess and Lianne had been best friends since at least the third grade. They liked the same kind of clothes. Sometimes they even dressed alike. And they both loved collecting stuffed animals. They met at the park every morning to walk to school, ate lunch together in the school cafeteria, and walked home together, too. Except today, Lianne thought. I'll sure be glad when that play is over!

When Lianne turned the corner at Bess's street, she could already see Bess sitting on her front steps. Her red pigtails were shining in the sun, and she was eating a big handful of cookies, one by one.

"Hey, Bess," Lianne yelled down the street. "Let's go to the park!" Bess stuffed the last of the cookies in her mouth and got up.

The kitten kept trying to stick its head out of Lianne's jacket. Lianne pushed it back in and tried not to giggle. Bess, huffing and puffing, hurried to where Lianne stood.

"Boy, do I have a surprise for you!" Lianne said when Bess got closer.

"What's up? Why didn't you wait for me after play practice?" Bess asked, wrinkling her freckled nose. She brushed cookie crumbs off her plump fingers. "Did your mom make your costumes yet? I can't wait till Mom finishes mine, especially my ball gown!"

"Come on! Let's go to the park! I have something to show you!" Lianne grabbed Bess's arm and practically dragged her to the corner.

Luckily, the park was still empty. Lianne sat on one of the swings. Bess plopped down beside her. Smiling at Bess, Lianne unzipped her jacket and pulled out the kitten. She thought Bess's eyes were going to pop out of her head.

"What—where—oh, I love it! Let me hold it!" Bess begged.

Bess grabbed the kitten and put it on her lap. "Where'd you get it? Hey, watch out!" One of Bess's pigtails was hanging over her shoulder. The kitten grabbed the yellow ribbon dangling from the end of it.

Lianne giggled as she tried to pull the ribbon away from the kitten. They played a short game of tug-of-war. Then the little cat let go of the

ribbon and curled into a ball on Bess's lap. Its eyelids slipped lower and lower and finally closed.

"I can't believe it! Is it yours? Will your mom let you keep it? What's its name?" Suddenly Bess stopped asking questions and sneezed, three times in a row.

"Oh, no! My allergies! Here! Take it! Take the kitten!" Bess shoved the kitten at Lianne and pulled a crumpled tissue out of her jacket pocket. She held it over her nose and mouth and started taking quick breaths, like she was going to sneeze again.

Lianne hugged the little cat, who was now wide awake and kind of damp, thanks to Bess's sneezes. "I found it right over there!" Lianne pointed. "In the trash barrel. It was trapped, and I saved it," she said proudly. "I'm going to call it Muffy."

"What about your Mom?" said Bess. Her face was getting blotchier by the minute.

"I don't know. I hate to even ask," Lianne

sighed. She looked at Bess pleadingly. "How can I get my mom to let me keep Muffy?"

Bess just looked at her through watery eyes. With a heavy sigh, Lianne glanced down the street at her house. She could barely see it, but she knew which one it was because of the huge oak tree that grew beside it.

"Wait a minute!" Lianne suddenly had a plan. One branch of the tree nearly touched her bedroom window. "If I can just get Muffy to climb that old tree, I can let her in my window! No one would know! That's it! Bess, I am going to have my very own cat!"

Four

THAT night Lianne went up to her bedroom early. She told her parents she was going to read. She closed her bedroom door and opened her window.

"Here, Kitty. Come on up!" Lianne called in a hoarse whisper. At first the only sound was the rustle of the few leaves left on the old tree. Then she heard a faint "Mew." "Muffy! Come on, Muffy! You can do it! Come on."

Lianne watched as Muffy scampered up the rough tree trunk. Then Muffy walked along the thick limb that grew toward her window. When the kitten was finally within reach, Lianne grabbed it. Whew! she thought. Safe at last!

The kitten licked Lianne's chin with a rough, pink tongue that felt like it was scraping her skin off. She laughed. "Ouch! That hurts!"

Just then there was a soft knock at her door. "Lianne, are you ready for bed?" It was her father!

"Almost!" Lianne shoved the cat under her comforter and lay down on the bed. She pulled the comforter up to her chin. Then she grabbed the nearest book and said, "Come in!"

"I just wanted to kiss you good night, honey," her father said. "What are you reading?"

Lianne looked at the book. "Uhh—my spelling book! We have a test Friday," she said quickly. Lianne could feel the kitten moving around by her feet. She bent her knees so that the comforter was spread out like a tent. This hid Muffy better.

"Do you want me to help you?" her father offered.

"No, not now. Maybe tomorrow. I'm kind of tired." Lianne let her eyes almost close. The kitten had the pant leg of her pajamas in its teeth and was pulling on it. Lianne was having a hard time concentrating on what her father was saying.

"Okay. Good night, Kitten."

Lianne's eyes flew open. How did he know? Then she remembered that he always called her "kitten." Keeping this cat a secret sure is tough! Lianne told herself.

"'Night, Dad," she said. "See you in the morning!"

As soon as her dad went out the door, Lianne reached under the covers for the kitten. Muffy chomped down on her thumb with needle-sharp teeth. "Ouch!" she said.

"Lianne!"

She dropped the cat. Her mom was standing in the doorway! The kitten leaped onto the floor and ran under the bed. So much for secrets!

"Where did you get that cat?"

"Uhhh . . . . Well, I—I was walking home from school and—and I heard this little noise and . . . ." The angry look on her mother's face made it hard

to talk.

Lianne gave up explaining and crawled under the bed to get Muffy.

"See?" Lianne held the kitten up for her mom. "It's just a baby. It doesn't have a mother." Lianne tried to keep her lower lip from trembling.

"Can't I keep it?" she begged. "I can take care of it. I'm old enough now! I want to adopt it, like you adopted me."

Lianne saw the angry lines on her mother's forehead disappear. Mrs. Bennett pulled her daughter up to sit on the bed and sat down beside her. "You know your father and I don't want any more pets, Lianne. We have enough to take care of with you and Amy and both our jobs."

Mrs. Bennett smoothed back the strands of shiny black hair that had escaped from Lianne's braid. "When you're grown up and have your own house, you can have as many pets as you want. This kitten can find another home."

"Maybe it will starve to death! Or get hit by a

car!" Lianne looked down at the tiny cat curled up in her lap. She swallowed hard and then asked in almost a whisper, "Who would have taken care of me if you hadn't adopted me?"

"You are a very special girl, Lianne." Her mother hugged her tightly. "Another family would have taken you home and loved you like we do."

Lianne's mother tipped Lianne's chin up so she could see her face. "But I don't know if anyone could love you as much as we do." Lianne felt hot tears behind her eyes.

"But I love this kitten!" she begged.

"Kittens are different from people. There are lots of kittens in this world, but only one Lianne," her mother said softly. "This kitten will find another home."

"But, Mom!" Lianne protested.

"You just can't keep this cat, Lianne." Mrs. Bennett picked up the sleepy cat. "Right now I'm going to put it back outside. If it's still around here in a day or two, maybe we'll take it to the animal shelter." She kissed Lianne's forehead and turned out the light.

"The shelter can find it a good home. Good night, honey."

Oh, no, thought Lianne as she lie in the darkness. She knew what might happen to the kitten if no one adopted it at the animal shelter.

"I'll find a way to keep you, Muff," she promised out loud. "I'll think of something! I won't let them take you to the animal shelter!"

Five

"WHAT happened? What happened?" Bess already was waiting at the corner park to walk to school with Lianne. "Did Muffy climb the tree? Tell me!"

Lianne stared at the sidewalk. "My mom came in my room and saw Muffy. She's going to take her to the animal shelter."

"Oh no!" Bess's eyes grew big and round. "What'll we do?"

Lianne looked up at Bess. "We have to hide Muffy," she said. "Then my mom will think she found a home!"

"Where? Not at my house! I'd be sneezing all over the place!" Just the thought of it seemed to make Bess's nose start running. While Bess fished in her jacket pocket for a tissue, the two girls slowly started walking toward school.

"Maybe you could still keep Muffy in your bedroom," Bess said hopefully. "How about waiting until your mom and dad are asleep? Then let Muffy in!"

"I can't stay awake that long." Lianne sighed and kicked a little stone out of her way. "Hey, I know! I could wait till after they kiss me." She smiled for the first time that morning. "They hardly ever come back in after that. That might work!"

"Sure! It'll work!" Bess smiled back. "I know it will!"

The girls turned down the wide sidewalk that led to the school's double front doors. "See you at lunch time!" Lianne called as they each hurried to different homerooms.

At lunch that day Bess and Lianne pushed their trays through the cafeteria line. Then they headed toward their favorite table.

"Tuna fish sandwich and potato chips today," Bess announced. "I guess I could save half my sandwich for Muffy." She looked at the sandwich again. "Well, maybe part of half. I'm pretty hungry, too." Bess looked at the big square of pink-frosted cake on her tray. "Boy, it's a good thing cats don't like cake!"

Lianne wrapped Bess's piece of sandwich and half of her own sandwich in her napkin. She put the napkin in the pocket of her skirt. "Maybe I can hide a bowl of milk in my room right after school," she said. "Then I can give it to Muffy later!"

"Yecch! Gross! How can you eat like that?" It was Jenny, sitting at the far end of the table. She was watching one of the sixth-grade boys eat the entire piece of cake from the school lunch in one bite. "Yuck!"

The boy smiled. Bits of cake fell out of his

mouth. Jenny tossed her mane of blond hair back and rolled her eyes up in disgust.

Lianne eyed Jenny's carrot sticks, little wedges of cheese, and crackers. She shook her head. "Poor Jenny! The school food isn't good enough for her. It must be hard to stay so beautiful."

Lianne leaned close to Bess. "You know, Bess, Jenny does eat sweet stuff. I see her sneak candy in class all the time."

"Really?" asked Bess. Lianne nodded knowingly.

"I think the teacher even saw her once," Lianne whispered, "but she didn't say anything."

Both girls turned to look at Jenny, but she was on her way out the cafeteria door. Just then the bell rang. Lunchtime was over.

"Don't forget about play practice!" Bess reminded Lianne as they hurried out of the cafeteria.

☆   ☆   ☆   ☆   ☆

In the auditorium after school Lianne slouched in her seat. She was staring at the other kids going through their lines on stage, but she was thinking about Muffy. Maybe Muffy won't be there when I get home, she worried. Maybe she really will find another family to live with.

"Lianne, could you join us on stage?" Mrs. Monk asked. Everyone was looking at her! With a burning face, Lianne climbed on stage and stood beside Bess.

"Cinderella" was on stage, too. Lianne noticed that Jenny had tied her hair back with a red bandanna. It still looked beautiful!

"May I try. . . ," whispered Mrs. Monk softly. Silence. She tried again, louder this time, "May I try. . . ."

"May I try on the glass slipper?" someone said. With a sick feeling in her stomach, Lianne realized the voice was hers, but the line was Jenny's.

At first no one said a word. Then Jenny folded her arms across her chest. She turned toward

Lianne. "Lianne," she said through her teeth, "what are you trying to prove?"

Mrs. Monk gave Lianne a puzzled look, but said nothing.

Lianne looked down at the floor of the stage. "Sorry," she mumbled without raising her head. Oh, boy, she thought, was that ever dumb! Maybe Mrs. Monk won't even let me be an ugly stepsister now.

"Well, let's go on," sighed Mrs. Monk.

Lianne paid close attention during the rest of the play practice. She listened carefully and said only her lines. The minute it was over, Lianne whispered to Bess, "Let's get out of here!"

Lianne grabbed her books and jacket and hurried out the side door. Bess rushed to keep up with her. At least Muffy won't think I'm stupid, Lianne told herself. Just please let her be there!

Six

LIANNE almost ran home. Bess gave up trying to talk and just panted along behind her friend. At her street Bess called. "Bye, Lianne!"

Lianne waved and hurried on. She was just turning the corner by the park when she saw her mother and sister pull into their driveway. Oh, no! she wanted to yell. Now I can't play with Muffy!

The evening dragged on forever. Muffy must be starving, Lianne worried. Maybe someone else has fed her and she's going to stay with them!

Finally it was bedtime.

"Good night, Mom!" Lianne called to her mother after she kissed her good night. At last, sighed Lianne. She quietly got out of bed and opened her bedroom window.

"Mew!" Lianne jumped back. The kitten was already on the tree limb, waiting for her.

"Oh, Muff! I'm so glad to see you!" Lianne whispered. She picked up the little cat and hugged her.

"Wait until you see what I have!" Lianne found her skirt on the floor and pulled the napkin out of her pocket. The tuna and bread had mushed together in one wet lump, but Muffy ate it all. Then she crawled under the bed to explore.

Suddenly an old, red rubber ball shot out from under the bed with Muffy close behind it. The kitten raced around the room, chasing the ball and pouncing on it. When it stopped rolling, Muffy batted it with her paw and went after it again. Lianne had to put her hand over her mouth so she wouldn't laugh out loud.

THUNK! The ball hit the wall, hard.

"Lianne, are you in bed?" her mother called.

"I just dropped my book."

She grabbed Muffy and got in bed. The kitten curled up beside her and yawned. Lianne could see tiny teeth inside the little pink mouth.

"Oh, Muff, I wish I didn't have to go to play practice ever again!" Lianne whispered. The kitten looked up at Lianne with one blue eye and one green one.

"Mrs. Monk probably wishes I wasn't even in the play. Maybe I should just quit." Muffy rested her head on Lianne's arm, sighed, and closed her eyes.

"I guess you think I'm okay, though." Lianne smiled. Muffy felt so soft and warm lying next to her. I just can't put you back outside tonight, Lianne decided. She reached over and set her radio alarm clock for 6:00 A.M. Then she turned the volume really low.

"I hope this works," whispered Lianne. She switched off the lamp beside her bed. Then she lie back down on the bed and put her arm around Muffy. Please don't let Mom or Dad come in to check on me tonight, she prayed.

Seven

IT was still dark outside when the radio suddenly started blaring music. Lianne jumped up, knocking the kitten off the bed.

"Oh, Muffy! I'm sorry," she whispered. Lianne quickly shut the alarm off. She scooped the little cat up and hugged it.

"I hate to do this, Muff." Lianne shoved her window open halfway. "But at least you got to stay in most of the night. Boy, did it get cold!"

She put the kitten on a wide part of the tree branch. Muffy just stood there blinking.

"Go on, Muffy." Lianne gave the kitten a little push and shut the window. "You can come in again tonight. I promise. Go on, now," Lianne said softly to the sad-looking kitten.

Muffy looked at Lianne for a second. Then she scooted down the tree tail-first, right past Amy's window.

Lianne sadly watched her go. Then she yawned and slipped back into her warm bed. In seconds she was asleep again.

"Lianne! Amy! It's time to get up. Hurry up!" was the next thing Lianne heard. She sleepily pulled some clothes on and squinted at herself in the mirror. She decided her hair didn't need rebraided this morning. A couple of bobby pins for the loose ends and it'll look fine, she told herself. Then she went downstairs for breakfast.

Amy was already sitting at the table, stuffing her mouth with cereal. Mrs. Bennett stood at the counter buttering some toast. Lianne's dad was still upstairs. Lianne could hear him talking to himself while he banged drawers open and shut. Probably looking for a pair of socks that match, she guessed.

What would Muffy like for breakfast? Lianne

wondered sleepily. Some milk, I bet, but how can I get it to her?

"Lianne, you have to try on your ball gown so I can hem it," her mother reminded her. "The play is next Tuesday. How about tonight after dinner? Okay?"

"Sure, Mom." Lianne did her best to sound excited.

Mrs. Bennett turned and smiled at her older daughter. "This is really going to be fun. You'll see!"

At least it will be over, Lianne thought.

Lianne had decided to wear her hair in a bun for the play. Her ball gown was a green velvet dress her mom had worn to a Christmas party. For the play, Mrs. Bennett had sewn beads around the neckline. Lianne thought it was too dark and old-looking. The weird hat her mother made with an old peacock feather sticking out of it didn't help either.

"But, Lianne," her mother had insisted, "you are one of the ugly stepsisters. The feather is

41

supposed to look funny!"

Lianne frowned at her cereal.

"Mom," Amy said between mouthfuls, "I saw the funniest thing this morning in the tree." Mrs. Bennett had turned back to the toast and didn't seem to be listening, but Lianne sure was.

"It looked like a . . ."

"Hi, Dad," Lianne said loudly, interrupting Amy. Lianne was sure she was going to mention seeing Muffy in the tree. "Did you find your socks?"

"Mumpf," he mumbled, reaching for a piece of the toast.

Amy turned to Lianne. "Did you see . . ."

"Your reading book? It's in the living room!"

"No, no. . . outside, in the tree!" Amy said. "I saw a little . . ."

"A bird! I saw it, too. Come on, Amy. You can walk to school with Bess and me today." Lianne grabbed Amy's arm and pulled her toward the coat closet.

"Boy, is it getting cold outside!" Lianne was

determined not to let Amy tell what she saw in the tree. "We need our winter coats today. Gloves, too."

"Winter coats?" Mr. Bennett repeated. He looked out the kitchen window. A yellow leaf fluttered down. "I swear winter starts earlier every year. I better put up the storm windows this weekend."

Storm windows! thought Lianne. How will Muffy get in?

Eight

FOR Lianne the rest of the week was crazy. The part she spent with Muffy—the nights— flew by. But during the day she was always sleepy. Between the play and the kitten, Lianne was just plain worn out.

The worst part was play practice after school. Jenny kept forgetting her lines. Even Bess was hard to take. She was so cheerful!

"Five more days!" Bess announced Thursday as they walked home after practice. "I can't wait, can you? Can you come over and see my ball gown? It's beautiful!"

Lianne couldn't believe how excited Bess could get over a dress.

"It used to be my mother's." Bess twirled around on the sidewalk as if she were wearing it. "She wore it to a wedding a long time ago. It's light blue with a layer of white lace over the skirt. I love the sleeves!" Bess stretched out her arms. "They're long and puffy and made out of the same lace."

Bess smiled at Lianne. The sun shone on her freckles. "If I didn't have to put a fake wart on my chin," Bess said, "I'd be as beautiful as Cinderella!"

Lianne remembered play practice the day before when Jenny brought her gown to show Mrs. Monk. Jenny's older sister had worn it to a prom. Lianne couldn't take her eyes off it. She thought it looked like a soft, pink cloud.

The top layer was shiny, like satin. Jenny's mom had pulled the satin layer up a couple of inches in four or five places all around the skirt and held it there with bows. Lianne could see layers of net and lace underneath. Matching pink bows on the shoulders trailed down the shiny satin sleeves. Lianne thought she had never seen anything so beautiful.

On Saturday morning, Mr. Bennett put up the storm windows. Lianne had hoped for warm weather. Then he might change his mind. But for the last few days freezing wind had whipped dead leaves into little tornadoes that followed her and Bess to school every morning.

Saturday after lunch Lianne helped her mother load the dishes in the dishwasher. "I haven't seen that little kitten," Mrs. Bennett said. "I wonder if someone took it in."

Lianne just kept handing her mother plates and cups, one at a time.

Mrs. Bennett sighed. "It really was cute, but kittens grow into cats." Lianne could see tired lines under her mother's eyes. "Then they're just one more thing to take care of. Do you know what happened to it, Lianne?"

"I don't know where it is, Mom." And Lianne hoped Muffy wouldn't be anywhere around when her mother and sister went out to the grocery store.

A little later Lianne stood watching at the kitchen window as her mom and Julie pulled out of the driveway. Muffy was nowhere in sight. Whew! sighed Lianne. Time to call Bess!

"Bess, we've got to think of something," Lianne said. She slumped down in the soft blue chair they kept by the phone. "Sooner or later someone is going to see Muffy outside. Then Mom'll take her to the shelter!"

"This is really a problem!" Bess agreed. Lianne could hear her crunching something. Potato chips, she guessed.

"Hmmm. . . ," Bess said thoughtfully. "Your mom mostly doesn't want another pet to take care of. Maybe you could prove you can take care of Muffy yourself," she suggested.

"But how? What could I do?" Lianne asked.

"I'm thinking, I'm thinking," Bess said. Lianne

could hear faster crunching noises.

Suddenly Lianne smiled and stood up. "Maybe I could take care of Boomer! All by myself!" she said.

"Like you took care of my goldfish last summer?" asked Bess.

"I told you I was sorry! Besides I'm older now!" Lianne insisted. "I can do it! I'm going to start right now. What could go wrong?"

Nine

"**B**OOMER! Here, boy!" Lianne already had his leash in her hand. "Hey, Dad!" Her father was working in the basement. "I'm taking Boomer for a walk!"

As soon as Boomer got outside, he started rolling in the leaves. Twigs and pieces of leaves tangled in his curly white fur.

Lianne knelt down to see if Muffy was behind the bushes. Then Boomer suddenly took off running across the yard. He pulled the leash right out of her hand!

"Wait! Boomer! You come back here!" Lianne yelled. Boomer raced through the neighbor's flower garden, dragging the leash. He headed right for the birdbath in Mrs. Powell's yard. Lianne couldn't watch!

Sure enough, Boomer knocked into the birdbath. It tipped over and fell, spraying Boomer and the yellow and white flowers with cold, dirty water.

"Yip!" Boomer yelped. But he kept right on running. Suddenly he stopped and lie gasping on top of smashed flowers.

Lianne pulled the birdbath back up. It looked okay to her, but the flowers under it were crushed. Boomer caught his breath and started to get up.

"You bad dog!" Lianne grabbed the leash. "Look what you've done to Mrs. Powell's flowers!" She looked up just in time to see her mom and sister pull into the driveway.

Lianne dragged the dog over to the car. "I took Boomer for a walk!" she said brightly.

Mrs. Bennett looked closely at the panting dog. Twigs and sticks were tangled in his used-to-be white fur. Muddy water dripped off his back.

"Wow! What a mess!" Amy said.

"Where were you, Lianne?" asked Mrs.

Bennett. "Is there a swamp near here I don't know about?"

First Lianne had to apologize to Mrs. Powell. Then she was grounded the rest of the day. When Bess called, Lianne wasn't even allowed to tell her what happened.

At this rate I won't be allowed to have a cat until I'm thirty-five! Lianne thought to herself.

At dinner Lianne pretended she wasn't hungry so there would be meat left for Muffy. It wasn't hard. The meat was liver. In fact, she seemed to be in a backward race with Amy to see who could eat the least liver.

After dinner Lianne took the garbage out, as usual. But before she stuffed the bag in the garbage can behind the garage, Lianne hunted through it until she found the leftover liver. Oh yuck! she thought. This stuff looks and smells even worse when it's cold!

"Here, Muffy," she whispered into the darkness. "Muffy! Look what I have!"

Lianne could hear leaves crackling. Then she

heard, "Mew! Mew!"

"Oh, Muffy! You're still here!" Lianne sighed with relief.

"Lianne! What's taking so long?" her dad called.

"I'm coming!" Lianne dropped the liver and ran to the house. When she glanced back, the kitten was chewing hungrily on the liver.

Later that night, after her parents had kissed her goodnight, Lianne got out of bed and went to her window. Muffy was standing on the tree limb outside the window, pawing at the glass.

Lianne tried to open the window, but she couldn't get the storm window to budge. She pressed her cheek against the cold glass. The kitten sat down on the branch and looked up at Lianne with hopeful eyes.

Nothing is going right, Lianne thought. Maybe Muffy should find another home. Then at least she'd have regular food and a warm place to sleep.

Finally the kitten curled up with her tail hiding

her nose and went to sleep, right there on the thick, rough tree branch.

The next morning when Lianne woke up, Muffy was gone. The whole family went to church. In the afternoon Mrs. Bennett took Amy and Lianne shopping for new winter coats. By the time they got back, it was dinner time.

Lianne ate a few bites of her steak and pushed the rest around on her plate. I must really love Muffy, she thought. Otherwise, I'd sure eat this myself.

After dinner, Lianne grabbed the bag of garbage and headed out the back door. In the freezing darkness she picked through the bag until she found her uneaten steak.

"Muffy!" she whispered. The only sound was the icy wind howling around the corner of the garage. Her fingers were getting numb. She held her arms close to her body to keep warm. "Muffy!" she called a little louder.

Then, through the darkness, she heard her mother scream.

Ten

LIANNE dropped the steak and raced into the house. Her mother was in the kitchen, leaning against the counter and holding one hand on her forehead. She was breathing hard.

Mr. Bennett stood nearby holding a wide-eyed Muffy by the scruff of her neck. Amy was standing in the doorway to the family room, staring open-mouthed at the kitten.

"Oh, it's just that cat!" Her mother's voice was a little shaky. "I thought a wild animal was in the house—maybe a giant rat!"

"Lianne, do you know anything about this?" Mr. Bennett asked quietly. He looked straight at her without blinking.

"She—she—must have come in when—when I went out," Lianne mumbled. "Please put her down, Dad. That hurts her!" Lianne reached out to take the kitten. But her father walked to the back door, set the cat outside, and closed the door.

"But Dad!" Lianne cried.

Mr. Bennett turned to his younger daughter. "Amy, you can go watch TV."

"But you said I watched too much TV already!" Amy protested.

"Amy, go in the other room," her father said firmly. Amy shrugged and went into the family room.

"Lianne, I told you that you couldn't keep that cat," her mother said. She pulled out one of the kitchen chairs and sat on it. "How do you explain that it's still here?" she asked.

"I . . . I . . . guess it hasn't found a home yet," Lianne said softly. She stared at the toes of her tennis shoes.

"Tomorrow after school we'll take it to the

shelter," her mother said. Lianne looked up at her mother in alarm. She wanted to cover her ears.

"No! We can't do that!" she yelled.

"Someone will come and give it a home," Mr. Bennett said gently. "It won't live through the winter outside, Lianne."

A tear rolled down Lianne's cheek. "I need Muffy!" She felt like the lump in her throat was strangling her. "I can take care of her. I promise!"

"You're just not old enough, Lianne." Mr. Bennett sat down and pulled Lianne onto his lap. "Have you already forgotten about the birdbath?"

"But, Dad! Cats are different. I can do it!" Lianne begged.

Mrs. Bennett sighed. "We'll compromise," she said. "Tomorrow I have to go pick up Grandma Bennett after school and the play is Tuesday night. We won't take the cat to the shelter until Wednesday. Maybe it will find a home on its own. But you can't keep that cat, Lianne."

"Thanks, Mom! Thanks, Dad!" Lianne hugged her dad and then reached over and hugged her mom.

Later, after her parents had kissed her and turned out the light, Lianne got out of bed and knelt at her window, staring out at the darkness. She couldn't see Muffy anywhere. At least I have two more days, she thought. Maybe a miracle will happen.

Just then her door slowly opened. "Lianne, are you awake?" Amy tiptoed into the room.

"Lianne, that's the same cat! The one I saw in the tree! Remember?" Amy knelt beside Lianne at the window.

"Yeah, I remember. I just wish I could keep her," Lianne said sadly.

"Me, too!" Amy said. "Can you see her down there?" Amy's breath was making clouds on the cold window. "I wish I could pet her. Or give her some milk. Cats like milk, right? What else?"

"Yesterday I gave her liver from dinner."

"You did? Cats like liver? Do they like lima

beans, too? She could eat mine!" Amy never liked anything they had for dinner. "She could have my salad, too!"

"Go back to bed, Amy." Lianne pulled her sister up and led her to the door. "Let me think."

Two more days, Lianne worried. That's not much time for a miracle.

Eleven

"LIANNE!" Bess yelled down the street. "Hurry up!" Bess was waiting at the corner park, hopping from one foot to the other in the chilly morning air.

"The play is tomorrow! Can you believe it's finally here?" Bess was talking a mile a minute. "I can hardly eat, I'm so excited!" Lianne could see strawberry jelly on Bess's cheek, so she knew Bess wasn't going to starve to death.

"Bess, help me . . . ," Lianne began.

"The Andersons next door are coming, too. To see me!" Bess was walking so fast Lianne had to run a few steps to keep up with her. "I hope I don't mess up!"

Lianne tried again. "Bess, my mom . . . ."

"I know, I know!" Bess interrupted. "My mom can't wait either!"

"Bess, my mom is taking Muffy to the animal shelter on Wednesday!"

Bess stopped so suddenly that Lianne bumped into her and dropped her school books.

Bess was finally listening. "Oh, no!" she said. "What happened?"

Lianne let the books lay on the sidewalk while she told Bess all about Muffy.

"Only two more days!" Bess said. "We've got to find Muffy a home! Fast!"

Lianne knelt to pick up her books. She looked up at Bess. "Bess," she began. "Couldn't you keep Muffy? Then I could still play with her sometimes. We both could!" she added quickly.

Bess shook her head sadly. "I'd like to, Lianne. I really would! But I can't. My allergies . . . . If Muffy were a goldfish," Bess said, "I'd take her in a second. My mom even likes cats!" She glanced down at her watch. "Hey, we're going to be late for school! Let's run!"

All through the school day, Lianne stared at teachers and blackboards and textbooks, but her mind was busy trying to think of a way to keep Muffy. Every plan she thought of had some major problem, mainly that her mom would never agree to it. When she finally got home after play practice, her mom met her at their front door.

"Lianne, do you want to come with Amy and me?" her mom asked. She gave Lianne a hug. "We're going to pick up Grandma Bennett."

Grandma Bennett was actually Lianne's great-grandmother. If you forget that I'm adopted, Lianne reminded herself. Grandma had insisted on coming to see Lianne's play. Grandma Bennett always knew exactly what she wanted.

"I'm kind of tired right now, Mom," Lianne said. She looked down at the books in her arms. "We practiced the second act three times today. I think I'll just stay here while you pick up Grandma, okay?"

Lianne knew she could play with Muffy while

her mom was gone. She forced herself not to smile.

"Well, you know the emergency numbers are by the phone," her mother said as she helped Amy button her coat. "We'll be back in half an hour or so."

As soon as her mom and Amy pulled out of the driveway, Lianne hurried out the back door.

"Muffy! Muffy!" she yelled. Where *was* that kitten? Lianne searched her yard and then the neighbors' yards. Finally she found Muffy at the corner park.

"Oh, there you are!" Lianne scooped her up and took her home. She got some tuna fish out of the refrigerator and went up to her room.

Lianne watched Muffy nibble at the tuna and then lick her face clean with her little pink tongue. "This might be our last time together, Muff. That stupid play will take all my time tomorrow." She picked the kitten up and cuddled it in her arms.

"Don't worry about the animal shelter," she

told Muffy. "Someone nice will adopt you. Maybe another girl will love you as much as I do." Lianne felt hot tears gathering in her eyes.

Then she heard a car pull into their driveway.

Twelve

THE front door opened. "Lianne, Grandma's here!" her mother called.

"Hi, Grandma! I'll be down in a minute!" Lianne tried to keep the panic out of her voice.

"Stay there, Lianne," Grandma Bennett called from the bottom of the stairs. "I'm coming right up to see your ball gown."

Lianne gave the window a desperate yank, but it still wouldn't open. She had to hide Muffy! Her sweater drawer was big enough! She scooped the sweaters out of it onto the floor. Lianne shut the surprised kitten in the drawer. Seconds later her great-grandmother tapped on the bedroom door.

"Come on in!" Lianne said. She turned on her radio, loud.

"Lianne! I'm so glad to see you, dear!"

Grandma Bennett was easy to hug. She wasn't much taller than Lianne and was even thinner. Grandma Bennett always smelled like powder. When Lianne was little, she thought her great-grandmother used powder to make her hair white.

"Well, Esmeralda!" Grandma Bennett slowly eased herself down on the edge of the bed. "Let's see your ball gown."

Just then Grandma sneezed. Oh, no! Lianne remembered. Grandma's allergic to cats, too!

"Do you have a cold?" Lianne hoped that was the problem.

"No, I can't say as I do. Maybe it's the change in the weather." Grandma Bennett took out a lacy handkerchief and patted her nose.

"Maybe you'd be more comfortable downstairs," Lianne suggested hopefully.

"But I haven't seen your dress yet," her great-grandmother insisted.

As Lianne turned toward her closet, she heard a muffled "Mew!" She turned the radio up.

"Here it is," Lianne said. She held the awful green dress up for her great-grandmother.

Grandma Bennett ran her thin hand down the soft velvet. "It's beautiful! Why, I remember when your mother wore that." She smiled. "It really looked beautiful on her."

Then she turned to Lianne, "Dear, does the radio have to be so loud?"

"It's my favorite song!" Lianne smiled brightly.

Grandma sneezed again. "My land, I don't know what's bothering my allergies." Her eyes were beginning to water.

"Mew!"

Grandma turned toward the sweater drawer. Lianne held her breath.

The old woman shook her head. "Music these days! It sounds so strange!"

Whew! thought Lianne.

Lianne's mother appeared in the doorway. "Dinner's almost ready. Let me help you downstairs, Grandma."

"I'll do fine on my own!" Grandma snapped.

"I'm not as old as you think!"

I'll be down in a second, Mom," called Lianne as the two women slowly made their way down the stairs. She closed the door to her bedroom.

"Mew! Mew! Mew!"

How am I going to get Muffy out of here! worried Lianne. Maybe I could put her in a bag and pretend she was stuff I was throwing away. I could carry the bag out to the garbage can and let her out behind the garage. But with my luck Muffy would meow her loudest just when I walked past Mom!

Or maybe, Lianne thought sadly, I could put her in a suitcase and run away from home. At least then we could be together.

Lianne took another look at the storm window. She noticed that it was held in place with four little metal strips along the sides. Lianne turned all four strips so they weren't touching the storm window. The window was loose! She carefully lifted it out and set it against her bed. Cold air rushed in, making Lianne's teeth chatter.

Lianne grabbed the noisy kitten out of the drawer and put her on the tree limb.

"Go on down, Muffy. Hurry now!" she said urgently, giving the cat a little push. This was no time for long good-byes.

Someone was pounding on her bedroom door. "Lianne!" It was Amy. "Mom says to come down for dinner. Right now!"

"I'm coming!" Lianne quickly put the window back in place and turned the strips to hold it there.

At dinner all everyone talked about was the play. Amy had invited two of her friends to come. Dad had his camera equipment ready. Lianne started to feel a little excited herself. The green dress did make her look at least thirteen years old. As long as she didn't wear the silly hat, that is.

That night Lianne dreamed about glass slippers and peacock feathers. In all her dreams she never even imagined what really happened the next night.

Thirteen

THE next evening Lianne's father took her over to the school an hour before the play began.

"Now don't worry about anything! You'll be great!" He draped her costumes over a seat at the front of the darkened auditorium and kissed her. "See you later, honey!"

"Lianne!" Bess yelled. Bess was standing in the hallway at the back of the auditorium, just outside the girls' restroom. She was holding her costumes in a jumbled pile over her arm. Lianne waved and walked back to talk with Bess.

"Can you believe it's finally time?" Bess asked excitedly, in a squeaky voice.

Just then Jenny came out of the restroom. She looked pale and she kept one hand on the wall. "Aren't you nervous?" she asked them.

"Well, a little," Bess said with a giggle. Lianne smiled, but said nothing.

"I just threw up," Jenny whispered. "Don't tell my mother or Mrs. Monk." She put her hand on her stomach. "I hope I can remember my lines!"

"You'll do okay, Jenny!" Bess said cheerfully.

Lianne had never seen Jenny look so bad. Jenny's hands shook when she pushed back her hair.

"Did you see where I left my costumes?" Jenny asked no one in particular. She wandered into the auditorium.

"Do you think she's all right?" Lianne asked in a whisper to Bess.

"Sure! It's just stage fright. Let's put on our costumes for the first act," Bess suggested.

"I left mine on a seat by the stage. I'll be right back." Lianne walked into the shadowy auditorium. She saw her pile of clothes in the first row. Then she looked closer. Wait a minute, Lianne said to herself. Those aren't my costumes. Her breath caught in her throat.

"Jenny!" Lianne turned toward the back hallway. "Mrs. Monk! Bess! Someone come fast!" she yelled.

Jenny was slumped over in the seat. She wasn't moving. Lianne wasn't even sure she was breathing!

Mrs. Monk, Bess, and most of the cast rushed in. Someone turned on the overhead lights.

"Oh, dear!" Mrs. Monk said. She turned to a teacher who had come to help with makeup. "Call an ambulance, please. And then call Jenny's parents."

"The Stuarts. I know them," the woman said. She rushed off.

Jenny's face was glistening with sweat. Lianne tried to swallow the big lump in her throat. "What's wrong with Jenny?" she whispered.

"Well," Mrs. Monk said, taking a deep breath. "Jenny has diabetes. She's had it all her life, but

she didn't want you kids to know. She must not have eaten right today."

Mrs. Monk looked up at the circle of silent children. "This is called an insulin reaction. It's caused when the sugar in her blood gets too low from not eating."

Mrs. Monk picked up Jenny's limp hand and held it in both of hers. "It's not as serious as it looks. She'll be fine as soon as she gets the right medicine." Mrs. Monk closed her eyes and shook her head. "I should have watched her more closely."

"Jenny threw up," Bess blurted out. "But she said not to tell you." Bess looked so scared that her freckles had almost disappeared.

The other teacher rushed back. "The ambulance is on its way. So are the Stuarts."

"Why didn't Jenny tell us?" Lianne asked. She saw Jenny's beautiful hair getting wet from sweat. "Is that why she eats candy in class? Because of the sugar in it?"

Mrs. Monk nodded. "Little pieces of candy

help keep the sugar in her blood at the right level. We teachers knew about Jenny's diabetes, but Jenny didn't want you all to think she was sick." Mrs. Monk looked at the worried faces staring at Jenny. "Or different."

Jenny moaned. Mrs. Monk patted her hand and said softly. "It's okay, Jenny. Your mom and dad will be here soon."

Lianne desperately wanted to be alone to sort things out in her mind. But first she had to be sure Jenny would be all right. She could hear the ambulance siren, faint at first, but quickly getting louder. "It won't be long now, Jen," she said gently. Lianne smoothed Jenny's hair back off her face.

Jenny's parents rushed in right behind the ambulance crew. Mrs. Stuart talked to them as they hurried to the front of the auditorium. By the time they reached Jenny, one of the paramedics was already looking in her emergency case for the right medicine.

"Why don't you kids go get dressed?" Mrs.

Monk said to the cast. The group hesitated and then turned one by one to go.

Lianne started toward the restroom. She didn't want anyone to see that she had tears in her eyes. "Lianne, would you stay here a second?" Mrs. Monk called. Lianne took a deep breath and turned back toward the group huddled around Jenny.

Mrs. Monk met Lianne halfway down the aisle. "Jenny can't be in the play tonight. You know all her lines, Lianne. Could you be Cinderella?"

Fourteen

LIANNE started to cry. She didn't even care who saw her. This is what she'd wanted all along, she thought. But she didn't want it this way. Jenny had worked hard to be Cinderella. It wasn't right.

"Jenny will be fine, Lianne." Mrs. Monk put her arms around Lianne and pulled her close. "Maybe if she hadn't kept her diabetes a secret, we all could have helped her through this excitement." She pushed Lianne back so she could see her face.

"Jenny's costumes should fit you. Do you feel up to it?"

"What about Esmeralda? Who will be

Esmeralda?" Lianne asked through her tears.

"One stepsister will have to be enough tonight. Maybe Bess could say your lines, too. Do you think?" Mrs. Monk asked.

Lianne nodded and hiccupped.

The play was a tremendous success. Just before it began, Mrs. Monk announced to the large audience that Jenny was ill and that Lianne was filling in. Mrs. Monk had to whisper Lianne's new lines to her only twice during the whole play. Bess remembered Esmeralda's lines and her own almost perfectly.

During the intermission before the last act, Lianne's mom slipped backstage.

"Lianne, we're so proud of you we could burst. I came to help you get ready for the last act." Her mom reached behind Lianne and pulled the ribbon off the end of her thick braid. Then she shook Lianne's hair out so that it fell in smooth waves.

When Lianne walked onstage wearing Jenny's pink gown, with her shiny black hair flowing

almost to her waist, several people in the audience started to applaud. At the end of the play, the whole audience stood and applauded. It seemed to Lianne that the clapping went on for hours.

Lianne felt so happy. She didn't even remember that Muffy would be going to the animal shelter the next afternoon.

Fifteen

THE next morning, for the first time, Lianne came down for breakfast with her hair unbraided. All during the meal and the excited talk about the night before, Amy kept staring at her.

Finally Amy asked, "Mom, can I let my hair grow like Lianne's?" She tugged at her wispy hair to make it longer.

Everyone laughed. Lianne hugged her sister and wondered why she had ever been jealous of Amy's short brown curls.

"Lianne, you come straight home after school today," said Grandma Bennett. "I want you to help me make some special cookies before I leave tomorrow."

"Sure, Grandma." Lianne suddenly became very quiet. This was the day to take Muffy to the animal shelter. She glanced at her mom, but her mother suddenly got up from the table and began stacking the plates.

The school day was a blur. Kids she barely knew said, "Great job, Lianne!" when she passed them in the hall. A second-grader stopped Lianne on her way to English class and whispered, "You were beautiful."

At lunchtime, just as Lianne and Bess reached the end of the cafeteria line, they saw Jenny sitting by herself at one of the tables. The two friends looked at each other and nodded. Without a word they walked over and sat down beside Jenny.

"Jenny, you should have been Cinderella last night," Lianne said. "You would have been great!"

Jenny smiled for a second and then stared at the bunch of grapes in her hand. "I should have

been more careful. I knew what could happen. I . . .
I guess I was pretending I didn't have diabetes."

Jenny looked up at Lianne. Her eyes had red
rims. "I just wanted to be like everyone else,"
Jenny said softly.

"You don't need to be like everyone else!
You're special!" Lianne said. She thought Jenny
knew that!

"You're special, too, Lianne. Bess, you are, too.
The play couldn't have gone on without you!"
Jenny smiled at them and wiped her eyes on her
sleeve.

After school that day Lianne still felt warm and
happy when she and Bess started to walk home.
But the closer she got to her house, the colder
she felt.

"Well, Bess, this is it for Muffy and me."
Lianne shuffled through the dead leaves.

"Lots of pets get adopted at the animal shelter,
Lianne." Bess assured her friend. "I bet Muffy
will be adopted tomorrow!"

At the corner park the girls waved good-bye.

Well, Grandma will let me play with Muffy till Mom gets home. Lianne thought. She'll understand. Lianne walked up her front steps and rang the doorbell.

Lianne waited. Boy, she told herself, Grandma sure is moving slowly. Lianne pushed the doorbell again. Nothing happened.

"Lucky I have my key with me," Lianne mumbled. She unlocked the door and went inside. Grandma's purse was on the table by the door. She must be here, Lianne thought. Why didn't Grandma come to the door?

Sixteen

LIANNE heard a faint sound. "Lianne. In here." Her grandma's voice was coming from the kitchen!

Lianne dropped her books and ran into the kitchen. Grandma Bennett was lying flat on the floor near the table. She raised her head to look at Lianne, but she didn't try to get up.

"Thank goodness, child. Help me up! This floor is too slippery for an old woman!"

Lianne saw a bowl of cold soup on the table. "How long have you been here, Grandma?" She knelt on the floor beside her.

"Oh, some time, I guess. Maybe since lunch. Help me up now."

Lianne put her arm under Grandma Bennett's thin shoulders. She started to help her up when her grandma gasped. Lianne eased her back down on the floor.

"Wait a minute, Lianne," Grandma Bennett whispered. "Just give me a minute."

"You could be really hurt, Grandma." Lianne was worried. Then she remembered the night before. "I'm going to call an ambulance!"

"No, no, don't bother with that. I'll be fine in a second. Just let me catch my breath," Grandma Bennett said weakly. Lianne watched in alarm as her grandma's eyes started to close.

She moved quickly to the phone and picked up the receiver.

"Lianne." Grandma Bennett opened her eyes. "I'll be all right in a minute. Never mind calling anyone."

Lianne put the phone down. "What can I do?" she asked. Grandma Bennett did not answer. Her eyes were closed again. Her chest barely moved when she breathed.

Lianne dialed the number listed on the wall. "We need an ambulance at 34 Walnut Street. Please hurry! My grandma needs help!"

"Don't try to get up, Grandma. Help will be here soon," Lianne promised. She ran to the front door and opened it wide so the ambulance crew could come right in. Then she rushed back to her great-grandmother. She could already hear the sirens.

The crew had Grandma safely on their rolling cart and were loading her into the ambulance when Lianne's mom and Amy pulled up. Lianne's mom got out of the car almost before it stopped.

"What happened? Are you all right, Grandma?" she asked frantically. Amy stood behind her with her fingers in her mouth and her eyes as big as saucers.

"Well, you know, I think I'll be fine, thanks to Lianne," said Grandma Bennett. "She really took charge. Wouldn't even do what I said, lucky for me." Grandma winked at Lianne.

"She'll have to have X-rays to see if anything's

broken," the paramedic said. "It's a good thing this little girl called us, though. It doesn't pay to take chances at this age."

"This age!" sputtered Grandma. "I'll tell you a thing or two!" Lianne was sure then that her grandma would be fine.

At the hospital the doctor decided that Grandma had only bruised some muscles and would be fine after a few days in bed. He did make her stay overnight in the hospital, even though Grandma said she was in better shape than he was.

Later that night the four Bennetts finally sat down for dinner.

"You know, Lianne, your mom and I had a talk on the way back from the hospital tonight," her father began. "That was a very responsible thing you did today, calling the ambulance even when Grandma told you not to."

He forked a chicken leg onto his plate. "We decided that anyone who could do what you've done in the last two days could take care of one small kitten by herself."

Lianne looked at him. "What?"

Her mother smiled. "You can keep that cat, Lianne. Do you think you could find it?"

Lianne forgot how tired and hungry she was. "Could I!" She jumped up from the table and ran out the back door.

"I'll help her!" Amy yelled on her way out.

Later that night, after a dinner of chicken and milk, a sleepy kitten curled up on the bed beside an even sleepier Lianne.

Lianne's mom kissed her daughter goodnight and gave the kitten a little pat. "Tomorrow we'll get some real catfood." She smiled and turned off the light. "You're quite a cat, Muffy. And you're quite a girl, too, Lianne!"